For Kay,
May you
find No mouse—
only joy in
your house!
With love,
Tawiell Johnson

W9-AVZ-117

Mooma and the Mouse

Written by Tansill Johnson and
Illustrated by Kate Johnson

Copyright 2012 by Tansill Johnson. No portion of this book may be reproduced in any format without written permission from the publisher.

978-1-883911-56-0
LCCN 2011904954

Edited by Tamurlaine Melby
Design by Tom Trenz

Belle Isle Books
www.belleislebooks.com

Dedicated to my husband,
Wayne, who has the ego of a
mouse, the heart of a lion, and is
the love of my life. TJ

Every morning when she wakes up...

... my grandmother, Mooma, likes to drink a cup of coffee. She goes to the kitchen, takes out her special cup and starts the coffee maker.

One morning last winter when Mooma went downstairs to make her coffee, she saw something strange on the kitchen counter. It was a little, gray, furry thing, and it was moving!

"What is **that?**"she wondered to herself.

She walked a little closer to the counter. The little gray furry thing had a tail and two little, black-button eyes.

"Oh my! Oh my goodness!" screamed my grandmother. "It's a **mouse!**"

She called for my grandfather, **"PaPa!"** He came quickly.
"What's the matter?" he asked.

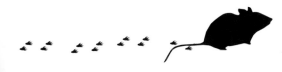

"There's a **mouse** in our house!"she yelled.

But the mouse was gone! Mooma and PaPa looked all over the kitchen. They looked high and low. They looked in things and under things. Mooma moved the cookie jar, the fruit bowl, two dishes and the breadbox. PaPa opened all the cabinet doors and all the kitchen drawers. Try as they might, they could not find the mouse. "What are we going to do?"asked Mooma.

"We will get some traps and catch the mouse. Don't worry,"said PaPa.

Mooma was very upset. "Oh, I do not like mice," she wailed. "They are **messy** and **dirty**. They belong outside a house."

PaPa explained that when it gets cold outside, mice try to find a warm place to live. "Our house has some very tiny holes. The mice find them and come inside. The hole can be as small around as your finger, but a little mouse can get through it."

That afternoon, PaPa went to the store and bought three mousetraps to set in different places in the kitchen. "This should do the trick," he thought.

PaPa set the traps out in the kitchen. He put
one on each end of the kitchen counter and
he put one trap on the floor in the corner.
On each trap he placed a little bit of food to
attract the mouse. He used pieces of cheese
and some peanut butter, too.

That night Mooma and PaPa went to bed.
Mooma was anxious to catch the mouse.
She did not like a mouse in the house.

The next morning Mooma and PaPa rushed to the kitchen. They checked the first trap on the counter. The food was gone, but **no mouse!**

They checked the second trap by the sink. The food was gone, but **no mouse!**

PaPa looked unhappy. The last trap was on the floor. He bent over to check it and saw that the spring had sprung.

The food was gone, but **no mouse!**

You see, the mouse had come in the middle of the night. He saw all the food and thought, "This family is so nice. They want to feed me. Usually I have to climb in drawers and chew through wrappers. This food is wonderful!"

"So, what are we going to do?"asked Mooma.

"We will try again tonight,"answered PaPa.

More determined than ever, PaPa set the traps with more food and once more placed them around the kitchen.

The next morning, they discovered the same problem. All the food gone and no mouse in sight!

Five more times they placed the traps at night and five more nights they fed the mouse.

On the sixth night Mooma told PaPa, "We are just feeding the mouse. **No more traps!**"

That night the mouse was very confused! All the food was gone. Even all the plates were gone. The mouse did not realize that the plates were actually traps. The mouse was hungry. In a nearby room, he found a basket of candy that PaPa always kept to snack on while he watched movies.

"Mmm," thought the mouse, "This looks tasty, too."

The next morning PaPa saw the mess the mouse had made in his candy basket. Boy, was he furious! PaPa took the basket of candy and put it in the refrigerator, where the mouse could not get it.

Soon the mouse realized that the people in the house did not like him very much. The food was always hidden and locked up tight. As the weather began to warm, the mouse began looking for a new home outdoors. When he found a place he liked, he packed his things and left out the same tiny hole he'd come through. "So long, house,"said the mouse as he went to his new home outside.

Mooma did not know the mouse had left. She looked for the mouse every time she went in the kitchen. Some days she thought she saw him, but it was only her imagination.

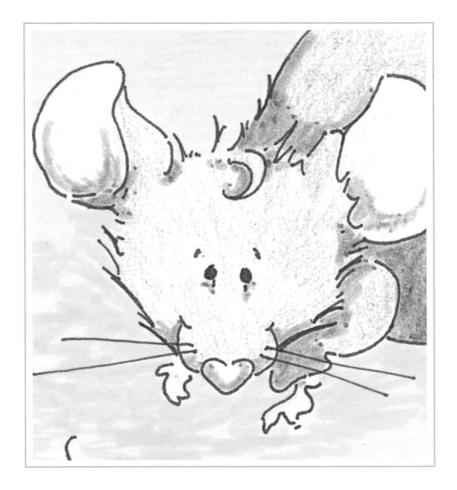

Mooma's adventure with the mouse was over.
At least until next winter...

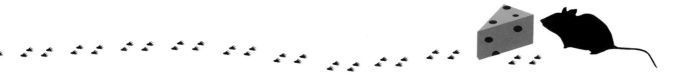